Learning to Read, Step by Step!

Ready to Read   Preschool–Kindergarten
• big type and easy words • rhyme and rhythm • picture clues
For children who know the alphabet and are eager to begin reading.

Reading with Help   Preschool–Grade 1
• basic vocabulary • short sentences • simple stories
For children who recognize familiar words and sound out new words with help.

Reading on Your Own   Grades 1–3
• engaging characters • easy-to-follow plots • popular topics
For children who are ready to read on their own.

Reading Paragraphs   Grades 2–3
• challenging vocabulary • short paragraphs • exciting stories
For newly independent readers who read simple sentences with confidence.

Ready for Chapters   Grades 2–4
• chapters • longer paragraphs • full-color art
For children who want to take the plunge into chapter books but still like colorful pictures.

STEP INTO READING® is designed to give every child a successful reading experience. The grade levels are only guides. Children can progress through the steps at their own speed, developing confidence in their reading, no matter what their grade.

Remember, a lifetime love of reading starts with a single step!

D0249702

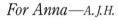

For Anna—A.J.H.

To my daughter, my pal, Kristen—J.M.

Text copyright © 2002 by Anna Jane Hays.
Illustrations copyright © 2002 by Joe Mathieu.
All rights reserved under International and Pan-American Copyright Conventions.
Published in the United States by Random House Children's Books, a division of
Random House, Inc., New York, and simultaneously in Canada by Random House of
Canada Limited, Toronto.

www.stepintoreading.com

Educators and librarians, for a variety of teaching tools, visit us at
www.randomhouse.com/teachers

Library of Congress Cataloging-in-Publication Data
Hays, Anna Jane.
Happy alphabet! : a phonics reader / by Anna Jane Hays ; illustrated by Joe Mathieu.
p. cm. — (Step into reading. A step 1 book)
SUMMARY: A phonics reader that uses rhyme and upper- and lower-case
letters to build alphabet recognition.
ISBN 0-375-81230-X (trade) — ISBN 0-375-91230-4 (lib. bdg.)
1. English language—Alphabet—Juvenile literature. [1. Alphabet.]
I. Mathieu, Joseph, ill. II. Title. III. Series: Step into reading. Step 1 book.
PE1155 .H4 2003   428.1—dc21   2002012967

Printed in the United States of America   12 11 10 9 8 7

STEP INTO READING, RANDOM HOUSE, and the Random House colophon are registered
trademarks of Random House, Inc.

HAPPY ALPHABET!
A Phonics Reader

by Anna Jane Hays
illustrated by Joe Mathieu

Random House 🏠 New York

A a
An **airplane** to fly.

Bb
A **balloon** so high.

Cc

A **cake,**
but why?

Dd
A **dinosaur** to ride.

Ee
An **egg** to hide.

Ff

A **fairy** with wishes
and **fishes**.

Gg

A **game** to share.

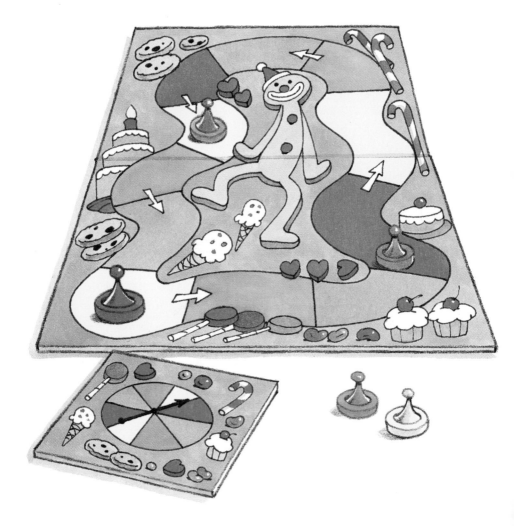

Hh

A **hat** to wear.

Ii

Ice cream to lick.

Jj
A **jellybean** trick.

Kk

A **kangaroo**
springing.

L l

A **lion** singing.

Mm

A **monster** in a vest.

Nn

An empty **nest**.

Oo
An **octopus** in a boat.

Pp
A **parachute** to float.

Qq

A **queen** on a throne.

Rr
A **rabbit** on the phone.

Ss

A **spider** spinning.

Tt
A **turtle** winning.

Uu

A **unicorn** swaying.

Vv

A **violin** playing.

Ww

A **witch** hot shot.

Xx

X marks the spot.

Yy

A **yo-yo** skipping.

Zz

A **zebra** zipping.

All have come
to the party today.

All are singing,
"Happy birthday!"

HAPPY ALPHABET!

Sing the alphabet.

Sing along

to the tune of

the birthday song.

One note for

each letter you get—

sing a

HAPPY ALPHABET!

A-B-C-D-E-F,

G-H-I-J-K-L,

M-N-O-P, Q-R-S-T,

U-V-W-X-Y-Z.